THE COMPLETE GUIDE TO SURVIVING THE TEENAGER

The Complete Guide To Surviving The Teenager

NL Riven

PennyLane
Press

Content

#Survival Notes IV: Trouble Shooting

Survival Mode

Do Not Panic

Do Not Shock

Proaction

Connections

Support

Go Wilde

#Survival Notes V: Recovery

I ♥ Tombies

Boonies

Five To Thrive

Words of Encouragement

Lastly

#Survival Notes VI: Afterwords

Words of Hope

Good Luck!

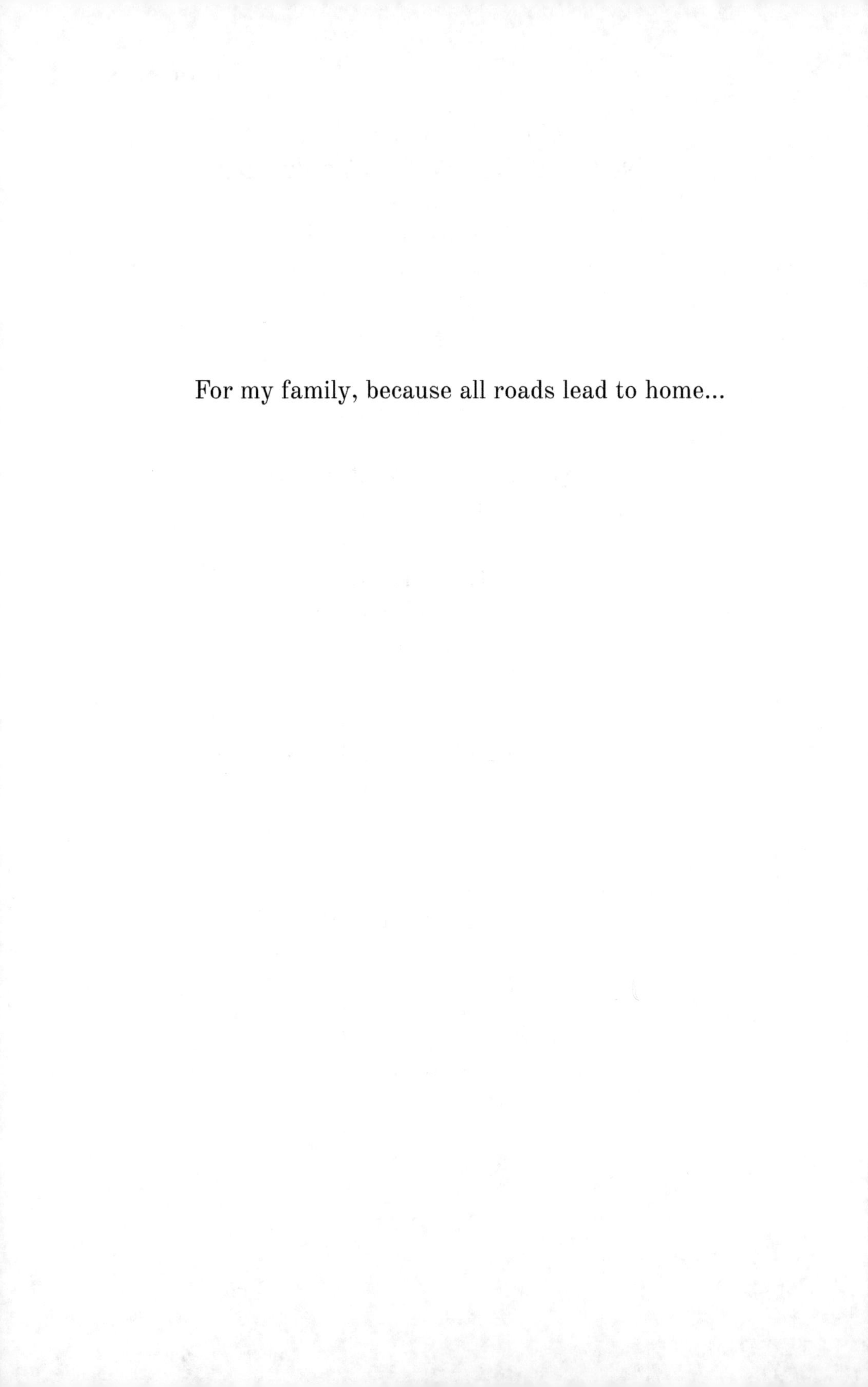

For my family, because all roads lead to home...

Survival Notes: Words of Rescue

Riven is an expert resource who shares practical tips and life-saving techniques in this latest installation, "The Complete Guide to Surviving the Teenager." These tools helped me fumble through understanding the diagrams of teenage wiring schematics.
- T. Taylor, A Man for the Handy

"Parents turning to this guide will find so much information packed in this book they should immediately shed their legwarmers and dress for success!"
-R.Williams, Pretty Woman

"I Heart Tombies" has changed my life forever!
- Olga, You've Made It Through Review

"If there is one word that comes to mind, it's unforgettable... Once you pick up this book, you cannot put it down. It is exactly what it promises- a literal shock and awe!"
-The Published Weekly

"This guide is full of the twists and turns that every adult, from the novice parent to the seasoned pro, needs to be aware of. The complete instruction manual can support anyone brushing up on the third law of teenage relativity, which postulates that the hormonal balance can crash down at any time or explode in the blink of an eye...
   - N. Ewt, Modern Science

"If you have a teenager, this book is a testimonial to the strength of character one must have to make it through adolescence. If you need extra support to muck it through, this guide will get you there!
   - The Muck Rack

Survival Notes I:
The Intel

1

DANGER

I repeat.
This is NOT a drill.
THEY will not only test you,
They will best you-
If *you* are not prepared!

With warnings of doom on repeat we may often wonder what Fifth Dimension world 'that' child originated from, because sometimes there seems to be no understanding of "that" adolescent species. These walking perplexions do not come with operating instructions or a money-back guarantee. A big warning label, yes, but no helpful cheat codes that offer instant enlightenment to the challenges of harboring an adolescent in your midst.

Luckily, you have found the most trusted authority on nearly nothing at all and resorted to this guidebook as your last-ditch resource. If you want to survive the most catastrophic events known to mankind, in other words, teenage PUBERTY, the only option is to hunker down with this safety guide in hand and muck your way through it. This survival series is dedicated to helping parents (such as yourself) in crisis, with some helpful hints for turning those dire emergencies into more peaceful engagements with your children.

You must pay close attention to the rules in this handy reference guide to help you boot up for oncoming events and safely walk away. Read the fine print, and DO NOT PANIC! With help, you will make it through the Wildes of PUBERTY, but you must be cautious, vigilant, and keep your guard up. Do NOT let yourself get fooled by displays of teenage grace and charm. Do NOT slip or show any signs of parental weakness, such as the adoring smile or slight hint of tears, or you WILL fall victim to wiley teens sprouting at every turn. T-R-A-P-T! There are no playbooks and no emergency hotlines to save you when spunky chunkies emerge as wild, teenage gremlins that act in irresponsible, irrational manners that you most certainly do NOT want to feed after midnight.

Observe the warnings, but do not delay! Discover hidden opportunities around every corner to support your new TEENAGER, and experience all the moments of chaos together. Not only can this guide help you navigate these thrilling events of PUBERTY, but it can also help you successfully transition your teenager into the real world beyond the Teencave. You can review the material in this guide at your own pace or during active crisis management. Feel free to stop and smell the poppies whenever you feel so inclined, but be wary if you wander too far looking for easy ways out. (Flying monkeys tend to get a bit cranky during winter months and are prone to using lost parents as bait.) You must start today and seize the limited-time opportunity to participate in the action-packed adolescent experience.

> **REMEMBER**
>
> Heed the warnings, but do not miss out. Puberty is a once-in-a-lifetime experience for your teenager, so take full advantage of this thrilling opportunity for the whole family!

2

When Moody Calls

Axiom Echo

Parents can begin preparing for the ultimate hormonal experience by reviewing the specifications of human children, for each child is wired differently with individual characteristics and personalities. As children mature- in or out of the fifth dimension- they become highly intelligent and often able to thwart their parental prey in battles waged of wit.

Preparedness will become an essential skill for parents in the everyday arena, and experience will gain you valuable knowledge. The arrival of the teenager into the home environment signifies the historic launch into a developmental time of human hormones, rapid physical changes, catastrophic mood swings, and reckless abandon. Teenagers can easily ignite mood disturbances in households, such as surges of slamming doors, decimated pantries, stinky socks, and pimple popping. Not all behavior is identified in limited warranty disclaimers, and different adolescent types can display variants of behavior.

As the job of a parent is not duty-free, there is most definitely a steep learning curve to any playbook of adolescence that you will have to learn and muck through as a parent. As you evolve during the path ahead, it will be wise to take the time to learn from the actions of your new teenager. This may be the most challenging hazard you have experienced yet, and you may get daily doses of shock therapy.

Recognize that during the most difficult (or rewarding!) days of catastrophe with your teenager, the struggle is not about you. In reality, neither are the rash arguments or door slamming. No matter how frustrated and angry you feel or how many times you take that door off, in the end, that teenager is still your carbon copy with a halo covered in adolescent muck. You cannot avoid it, and you cannot outrun it. So embrace the gifts of adolescence and enjoy this limited-time opportunity for your entire family with a black-tie event. Your mission, should you accept it, is to make it to the other side of puberty when Moody comes calling.

REMEMBER

You cannot avoid it, and you cannot outrun it.
Accept, embrace, or maybe even host a black-tie party for
the excitement that is thundering your way!

3

Hazards

Understanding the hazards of adolescence can help parents manage and effectively neutralize any threats to successful transformations. It is suggested that parental action teams be proactive, rather than reactive to crises, and develop care plans for transitional teens. Each day will dawn with new challenges that your teenager will fight with renewed angst, regardless of which direction the wind is blowing. In most cases, until teens can decode the mysteries of humanity, they may lash out in unpredictable and hazardous manners.

In one extreme case from Ohio, a wild teen was observed to have erupted in spontaneous flames and complete cranial rotation when enraged—an excellent reason to be prepared with heat and thermal-resistant equipment at all times. (Ned's Backwood Bargains is the perfect place for some holiday shopping! Find it here at www.neds-backwoods.com)

For the proper care and safekeeping of the hormonally challenged, essential highlights from the Parent Instruction Manual are referenced here (just in case a canine consumed your copy).

- Your teenager should be fully compliant with the UE, UCK, HACKI, and ENUF legislation.
- Do not short-circuit with periods of extended use or ancient language.
- Keep away from fire, it will get burned.
- Will work only with gluten free, triple pump, and fat free latte (double shot not included)
- Do not place close to unsecured food sources without proper protective equipment, or risk loss of fingers.
- Outerwear can be sterilized, but protective equipment must be used to remove sources of odor and food contaminates.
- For regular cleaning completely immerse in water, and ensure proper sanitary procedures are followed to remove all sources of biological warfare.

- Do not try to disassemble electronics if experiencing loss of power. Please contact customer service.
- Should this model be affected by local tween group interference, use 'grounded' or 'removal from group tactic'. Reset to achieve desired behaviors.
- Warning! Should any additional hormonal catastrophes be released, you will need to seek shelter immediately in a safe location that is at least 50 feet away from any identified Teencave. Once the immediate threat weakens, you may safely resume pre-crisis activities.
- For customer support or warranty questions, please contact 1-800-NOT-ITTT

OH, AND...

DO NOT EVER..

Feed Them After Midnight.....

EVER....

4

Forget Normal

As your teenager wades through the hormonal stages, you may question whether certain behaviors you have observed are expected during this transitional time or what you have experienced are normal caregiver reactions. Let me assure you that the state of normality during adolescence is always in question and seems to embrace a state of constant change. Once upon a time, high society may have imposed specific standards of conduct, but the people of today have spoken, and normal is no longer the norm.

As teenagers mark their way through puberty, attempts to adjust to variations of societal norms can result in rocky transitions to adulthood. Even though there is a general understanding that most parents can expect a few acts of malarkey from their teenagers during this transitional age, some adolescents turned wild teens on the fringes can push tomfoolery to extremes.

Not only have these wild teens created a surge of panic among their parental action teams, but many of these highly classified individuals have persuaded mobs of loyal followers to act out in rebellion against the homeland. **But again, do not panic!**

..YET...

5

Just Plain Malarkey

Axiom Echo

How does one gauge what "normal" teen behavior is if the rules continue to change? Research teams identified patterns of behavior considered "right," "normal," and "abnormal" by today's social Yoohoos. According to Zoltar "normal" is not a word that registers in a teen's vocabulary or "slays" in the typical dictionary of acceptable phrases. Table *Just Plain Malarkey-1* illustrates behaviors observed at selected stages throughout growth and development. Categories show that there are certain behaviors that many teenagers exhibit, such as slamming doors, pimple popping, and side-eye, that are rated as "normal" teenage behavior. Other behaviors assessed, such as fashion flops and pantry assaults, could be rated more as general malarkey.

Hormonal angst- rash acts such as ballroom dancing, bingo binging, potato popping, and even lion wrangling- are all escapades of buffoonery running wild through the streets of abandon. In most cases, this is not because your teen has lost his head, so hold on to your knickers. It is merely an adolescent's lack of maturity to make the decisions that society expects to be "normal," "appropriate," or the "right" decisions. It all looks like a bunch of malarkey to me! Am I right?

The concern would be for those wild teenagers who engage in elevated risk type activities, such as moonwalking or fire breathing, to challenge social norms and push past personal boundaries. These teenagers turned *Wildteens* may act irresponsibly, engage in scandalous behaviors, or even use copious amounts of facial products.

NOT THE HAIR GEL! ANYTHING BUT THAT!

JUST PLAIN MALARKEY- 1

Behaviors	Normal /Abnormal	11- 18 Yrs	18- 22 Yrs
Attitude	N	X	X
Swashbuckling	N	N	X
Side Eye	N	N	X
Cranial Rotation	A	A	A
Spontaneous Eruption/FireBreathing	A	A	A
Huffing, Puffing	N	N	A
Fashion Flops	N	X	X
Door Slamming	N	N	X
Pimple Popping	N	N	X
Pantry Raiding	N	N	N
"Teenpack Syndrome"	Yep!	N	X
Isolation/ Avoidance	N	X	X
Mood surfing	N	N	X
Moonwalking	The Moon?!!	A	A
Shenanigans	N	N	X

Buffoonery	N	N	X
Lion Wrangling	Nope!	Nope!	Still Nope!

6

Rising Rates of Buffoonery

Based on the data breach compiled by The RaisaRuckus Institute, approximately 1 in every three adults succumb to an unforeseen practical assault. In a worst-case scenario- extreme acts of buffoonery under hormonal duress. Playing 'dead' is a favorite ruse that always nabs an untrained parent- others such as wacky black brownies, potato cannon blast, and porch pooper plop are popular shenanigans used by extra wily ones.

As part of ongoing efforts to handle hormonal assaults more effectively, the OBeOne Organization rescues parental action teams that need crisis intervention and management of extreme acts of buffoonery. They offer training classes with elite masters, and it is highly recommended that endangered action teams have specialized training in deflection techniques before surges escalate.

FOR YOUR REFERENCE, LISTED HERE ARE THE TOP ACTS OF BUFFOONERY:

- Playing Dead- Falling for this ruse will land you in grave danger.
- Tears- Avoid any eye contact!
- Parent TRAPT
- Lost Phone Call
- Trojan horse
- Car Wrapt
- Smoking Toilet
- Porch Pooper Plop
- Wacky Jack Brownies

- Wifi 911??
- Egg-Stravaganza
- Forked Again
- What the Duck?

7

Fire and Brimstone

As the data suggests, one can not make assumptions regarding teenage behavior, for rebels push past the boundaries of right or wrong to ensure nonconformity. As moody behaviors surge, it becomes critical to a parent's sanity that in any engagement with a teenager, you absolutely forget what you have EVER learned about what "most people" would do. It does NOT matter what most people would do, or what society believes your teenager "should" do. It does not even matter what your child USED to do, or the patterns of behavior that your teen USED to exhibit. The ugly truth of the matter is that your child is now a TEENAGER, and you are faced with having to cope with the behaviors of this TEENAGER. The odds are your newborn teenager no longer speaks in a polite, polished tone with shiny new shoes, nor wishes to hide calmly in the shadows. Nessie has trudged out of the lake with her arsenal of fire and brimstone. Normal does not exist in your vocabulary any longer.

Attempts to rationalize and "dialogue" calmly with a teenager are highly improbable. Hormones, irrational behavior, and tempers engage teenagers in ways that keep them inept at holding a rational conversation. You would have a better success rate holding a sensible conversation with a mountain lion, so please do NOT try it at home. Do NOT attempt this with your tween, and do NOT engage them one-on-one without a safety partner.

As teenagers progress through the latent stages of adolescence and are better able to grasp their new mental and physical abilities, they become better able to communicate their own needs with others around them (including you).

REMEMBER
Forget "Normal".
It no longer exists.

Survival Notes II: The Training

8

Rules of Etiquette

In spite of the fact that teenagers are still amateurs in the game of life, parents must tread lightly when it comes to providing ancient words of wisdom to their snarky proteges. Regardless of how it develops, teenagers become very protective of their self-image and social connections. We may think of this as complete tomfoolery, but it does not matter in the slightest to the hormonally challenged. There are specific rules of etiquette that you, as a parent, must follow to maintain positive relationships with your teen and prevent a parent-induced catastrophe from striking.

- **Unacceptable**: The fashion ditch and switch may be a new trend in acceptable teenage behavior, but that wardrobe emergency of yours is not. Show up to school in that unsightly ensemble, and your tween will ditch you for a more fashionable model.

- **Illegal**: Vintage and eclectic threads from any yesteryear that conflict with the modern sense of fashion. For example, it is not acceptable to be seen wearing yesterday's brand of yoga pants, A.K.A. "mom" pants. Be forewarned, if caught wearing them, your teen may leave you stranded with a hungry pack of Tombies- and a hangry pack of Tombies is nothing short of terrifying!

- **Prohibited**: Use extreme caution when reaching for any item three sizes too small. This is the gentle reminder that your teen will disown any parent who attempts to sqqqqquuuuuueeeezze every possible extra inch of fluff into the latest pair of low risers, skinny jeans, or even athletic pants under the pretense of "running." This is unacceptable parental behavior, even if it is common practice for tweens to use the dirty hamper as a last-minute stitch fix.

- **Burn immediately**: Fashion toxins such as mom pants, stretchy joggers, hip-hop fanny packs, peg pants, toe socks, rat tails, scrunchies, suede jackets, fuzzy shoes, snowman vests, and anything else of the like. These fashion emergencies are easy targets for cranky twitches.

- **Unsightly**: I am genuinely sorry, parents, but the fact is that your hair is balding, and your teen thinks you are now 'uncool.' The fashion police have stipulated that a hat must be worn to any community space or accompanying your teen to any public event.

- **Outlawed**: Absolutely NO Twinnings! Dressing or acting like your teenager to fit into their social spheres is expressly prohibited.

- **Banned**: Any and all use of emojis, bitmojis, social butterflies, riz, and Chatgp lingo. Stop immediately, for your own sake! You are not twelve anymore, and they will remind you daily until you avoid entering their sacred digital space.

- **Restricted:** Use extreme caution when in teen common areas such as the street, kitchen, family room, shopping areas, school, town squares, sporting events, etc. Avoid these areas altogether, or your appearance will give your wild teen the perception of being overbearing, spying, or party crashing and will increase agitation. (Black market techniques of sneaking, snooping, stalking, or creeping are only permissible under Revised Code 043.201)

- **Strictly forbidden:** Forms of communication that include such harassments as 'Hello,' 'Goodbye,' or even the infamous 'How was school.' Momma Bear Hugs, Grandma kisses, Dad jokes, and obnoxious phone calls are not allowed and are punishable by an immediate vote off the island.

- **Observe:** Separation issues typically only appear for parents later in the teen stages; teens generally choose not to own any outward signs of affection for fear of rejection from their social spheres. Even though this is a generality, it is not an absolute, and a sign of affection from a teen can show up when least expected. Sometimes, a nod, a hug, or even a fist bump can slip out, causing significant confusion.

PRACTICE

View your teens at a distance. Respect their space, and cele-brate small victories at least two hundred feet away. Success does not happen overnight, but alas, there is *hope!*

9

Seek thee TEENCave

Seek thee TEENCave and

Thee shall find.

Many parents have helped their wild teens successfully muck it to the other side, having safely identified the location of a teen's lair. During adolescence, this location serves the teen as a place to self-isolate during hormonal sieges, periods of angst, and defensive positioning. Slamming of the lair door does not necessarily mean you have been outplayed; you must simply learn when the right time is to raid the bat cave (aka *TEENCAVE)*. You can effectively use the Teencave to your advantage if you keep in mind the following tips:

- **Remember**: The Teencave is often a place of safety and shelter for teens transitioning to adulthood. Teenagers have been known to take refuge in the Teencave for hours at a time, often leaving only for basic survival necessities such as FUD, hydration, or Teen*pack* activity.

- **Warning**: Any time you do not respect this adolescent space, they may react in hostile ways. It may smell bad, fraught with unrecognizable layers of polyester, but your teen has deemed the Teencave as safe territory. As such, if you dare to enter, prepare to feel the full brunt of hormonal angst. If a teenager has marked their territory with a big red " Get Out" sign, the Surgeon General recommends a hasty retreat before your head is lost forever.

- **Beware**: Some teenagers can become so lost in a self-quarantined hibernation that they do not see the light of day until their immediate crisis has ended. These teens can, at times, hibernate in their self-quarantined caves for lengthy periods. This is most likely an issue with your Teen Zombies (TOMBIES), who are especially susceptible to these risks during Stage I Dormancy. These teens, turned *Tombies*, plunge into semi-catatonic states of hibernation that could include extended periods of media gameplay, TV watching, social networking, or binge eating. It is entirely possible that given an extra large pizza and a fully charged cell phone, a Tombie could disappear into a teen cave for an entire weekend. The only exception might be large teen gatherings at the square, a harvest moon, or a Mumu sale at the Mall.

- **Danger**: Do not be distracted by the shenanigans of a clever Tombie, especially a hungry one at that. You may witness one snoring on the floor, but a sniff of pepperoni pie will send a novice Tombie into a feeding frenzy with limbs askew. In these cases, extreme caution should be used when delivering carryout. It is suggested that proper equipment, such as the extended-length poking stick, be carried at all times, and feeding times must NEVER be administered after midnight.

- **Hint**: Although maddening, allow teens this time to take refuge in the Teencave away from the atrocities of the outside social sector. If cause is necessary to remove teens from the lair, work collaboratively with your action team to draw the teen out of the Teencave before decontamination, raiding, or looting. Try using FUD to draw hangry teens away from the Teencave while a partner secures the area. Another strategy proven effective utilizes a ringtone to distract, disorient, and even draw your Tombie into more neutral areas away from looting grounds. As a general rule of safety, raid only when necessary and leave no evidence.

REMEMBER

When in doubt,
Seek the TeenCave, and
Thee shall find.

10

Speak Fluent Teen

During extended periods when it becomes difficult for parents to understand the language of a teenager in a helpful way, the ability to communicate on some level and understand the needs of your wild teenager specifically will be critical for the survival of your sanity. It can be highly beneficial for support teams to learn the teenager lexicon, but this must be applied only in cases where traditional communication has failed. Ensure to dialogue with care and be mindful of the language you are attempting to speak. It may be helpful to keep the following strategies in mind:

- **Tip**: Teenagers tend to speak in their primary *"Teenspeak"* language, rather than proper native grammar. As various dialects and accents are associated with this "Teenspeak" lexicon, it can be challenging to learn and speak "Teenspeak" in a way that is helpful for adults. Parents who can learn to communicate effectively in the "Teenspeak" language will be able to engage in more positive relationships with their teenagers. Grunts, huffs, scowls, and even bits of *Buffoonspeak* are encouraging scraps of communication that build the foundation to complete sentences.

- **Hint**: Take care of the verbiage you are attempting, with the hope it does not backfire on you as you learn to communicate with your teen. That 80's slang you keep trying to use will cause a scene with the *cool kids*—definitely not a winning situation.

- **Suggested**: In some cases, additional research on updated terminology in social media would be prudent for learning effective methods of communication with your teen. Continued education on the letters of FB, X, TikTok, LOL, IPod, XBOX, Meta, IDK, ZOOM, and other yellow bricks of social distraction would be beneficial in situations of extreme teen Instagramming.

- **Caution**: Buyer beware! Not only does your teen have the extra sensory perception to sniff out the nearest Armani sale, but they can also sense truthful or misleading communications in your offensive tactics. Yucatan mind meld tactics are not recommended in this case.

- **Warning**: As noted, attempts to rationalize and dialogue calmly with a teenager should not be taken carelessly. If you are not entirely comfortable using these Teenspeak tactics with your teenagers or need assistance learning the correct forms of modern Teenspeak, please seek additional guidance from a trusted Teenspeak professional. In extreme surges, calm dialogue with your teen may not be possible. Mood surges may escalate, reaching higher category levels and forcing your parental action team to engage in new tactics.

PRACTICE

Teenspeak is a highly evolved lexicon and is only effective when used properly. Start with entry level words, then advance to more complex dialogue.

11

Speak Fluent FUD

Do not, under any circumstances, underestimate the influence that food and shelter have on your teen's basic survival pyramid. As a parent of a Wildteen, it is vital that you learn to speak fluent FUD. You may find that your teenager has individualized needs, requiring a more specific care and feeding regimen. If not cared for appropriately, wild teens can be more susceptible to many serious problems, including extreme bouts of mood swings. Experts recommend the following:

- **Monitor:** The dietary needs and/or restrictions of Wildteens need to be monitored, as the teenagers can become malnourished or severely moody if fed improperly. These junk food-binging mammals prefer to hash out on high-calorie and processed foods such as fast food, coffees, sodas, and energy drinks- often leaving more nutritious and organic foods for the family canines. One must take extra care when prepping or storing foods; teens cannot distinguish food from wrappers or foils and can get sick if consuming these foods at ultra-fast binging speeds.

- **Safety First:** It is essential for **your** safety that you do not look teens straight in the eye while they are feeding and that you back carefully away from the feeding ground. Some wild teens can become agitated during mealtimes and can become aggressive if not de-escalated with calm words and appropriate nutrition. Remember to wear proper protective equipment at all times and always have your safety partner with you.

- **Hint**:   Use of the extended-length poking stick can be used as protective equipment for the feeding of multiple teens or in cases of extreme hunger.

- **Restricted**: Feeding in large numbers can lead to public health concerns. Too many junk food-binging teens in one zone can increase the likelihood of noise pollution in quieter neighborhoods and among other wildlife.

- **Caution**: Do NOT allow food scraps to drop onto the ground, and do not allow "the ten-second rule" to apply.

- **Warning**: Do NOT place leftover meals and snacks in the refrigerator or unprotected cabinets. Instead, use sealed containers with teen-proof lids stored in unreachable spaces. Anything edible within a teenager's reach is "fair game" and bound to be your loss.

- **Suggested**: Keep single-use Bigbucks coffees or other beverage containers available at all times. A stocked arsenal means you are less likely to find milk and juice containers drained on the refrigerator shelf.

- **Observe**: Increased fitness will decrease agitation and aid in better sleep patterns. Use gerbil wheels or similar mechanicals for those wild teens that exhibit more intense energy patterns.

- **Strictly forbidden**: Absolutely, Positively, must abide by the NO food of any kind after Midnight rule. A broken rule will result in catastrophic consequences- DO NOT ATTEMPT IT!

Speak Fluent NO

Do not panic, fear, or by any means let yourself play the victim in engagements with your teenager. Bolster your defenses and practice the 'NO' mantra- 'No' that remains absolutely **not open for discussion**. Whether it is a battle waged over the chunky monkey or the day's fashion ensemble, parents must always be the victors of the spoils and must never give in to any ransom negotiations with children. -N- O- **Do not let it happen**. No bribing, tears, giant blue eyes, pony tricks, white flag. Ever! Should you find yourself in a position where your teen is attempting to negotiate a ransom for the release of your Snickerdoodles, you must stand. Under no circumstances should you attempt to haggle with your child, as the likelihood of you winning the battle decreases with each huff and puff. Teenagers have learned to be excellent strategists and are highly successful at manipulating lightweights.

Acting with respect and following rules of engagement, even when saying "NO," can decrease the likelihood of counter acts of buffoonery. If you have been a lightweight in the past, a peacemaker, a healer, a victim of defeat, or a tender soul- saying 'NO' could be very difficult for you. As a parent, you need to be able to identify precise boundaries. If someone crosses that line, including your teen, it is acceptable and necessary for you to enforce the word NO respectfully! Not only should your teen respect and obey your boundaries, but **you,** as the parent, should also play your part by enforcing the "NO" objective with concrete actions. Absolutely no haggling for your Snickerdoodles! No battles, no negotiation, no arbitration.

N-O

13

Be A Player

Parenting is hard; we get it! TEENS are wild, we know!

Buttttt remember that under no circumstances should you ever give up your control, give in, admit defeat, or admit that children can be outright terrifying at times. It may seem obvious, but children of all ages are known for being especially twitchy at preying on a parent's temporary weakness. It only takes a split-second lapse in control, despair, confusion, or lack of knowledge before one has become a victim of teenage target practice.

Be prepared when doom attacks. Do not play the victim—be a player! The more knowledge and strength you can gain from ancient warlocks will help you get back in the game and prepare the most effective strategies. Stand up, straighten your hairpiece, and be ready.

REMEMBER

Do NOT play a victim.
Be a Player

14

Do NOT Be A Victim

Axiom Echo

Building a solid foundation of survival skills, following proper etiquette protocols, and completing further competency training can decrease parental lapse of control and increase positive engagement. Parents who incorporate skills into their daily routines and make efforts to tune into their teens' specific language and needs have more successful encounters.

On the other hand, an underlying current of angst can develop in the family dynamic if engagements are not favorable. Once a door is slammed and the herd has stomped up the stairs, peace treaties may be disrupted until a successful solution can be initiated. If a wedge continues to divide instead of conquer, tensions can increase along with major acts of mischief.

Symptoms of adolescent burnout can develop with feelings of anxiety, resentment, and even jealousy. There are no shiny yellow brick roads to take here. Just good old-fashioned goop, sweat, and ridiculous amounts of teenage body odor.

NEED HELP? FIND OUT HOW!
CLIFF NOTE VERSION
HERE!

Survival Notes III: Active Engagement

15

The Survival Gear

Caution: Do not poke the bear!

Axiom Echo

To train properly against rising acts of buffoonery, you must also be armed with the most appropriate battle gear. It is essential to know which gear is permissible and which equipment is restricted. Certain types of weapons are universally banned (or just considered bad form), such as silver bullets, garlic grenades, and fruitcakes. Others, such as nano missiles, stink bombs, potato cannons, and firecrackers, are permitted with mature audiences only.

Authorized forms of weaponry may include:

- **Poking Stick**: A long wooden stick measuring approximately 10 meters, used as protective equipment and defensive weapon. When utilized effectively, the poking stick can be a multi-tool used as a warning device, sleeper shocker, food flopper, potato popper, pathfinder, rubble rooter, chubba thwumper, or stick in the mud.

  *Err on the side of caution and do not poke 'The Bear', as some bears tend to have short tempers and fits of fury.

- **Potato Cannon (*Prior authorization needed)**: For practical use, the potato cannon is easy for adults to assemble. It is a pipe-based cannon that uses air pressure or flammable gas to launch small projectiles. These can be built around residential perimeters as defensive weapons or to fire chunks of potatoes and other small objects as an offensive tactic. Prior authorization is needed to use these cannons around perimeters, as projectiles can be launched long distances into neighboring windows, gardens, or passing patrol cars.

- **Pumpkin Chucker:** The pumpkin chucker is similar to the potato cannon in its methodology but different in design. A chucker weapon is designed to sling a pumpkin or similar-sized objects by mechanical means. It can be similar to a catapult, trebuchet, etc.

- **Nano Missile:** These miniature missiles pack a powerful punch and can easily knock your socks off. Your gremlins are known to be particularly fond of causing chaos with these little bits of nanotechnology.

- **Stink Bomb:** No explanation needed. If grandma's cooking, take cover and hope for the best.

- **Fruitcakes (Not Recommended):** Densely packed with nuts and berries, these indestructible baked goods are truly weapons of mass destruction in the wrong hands.

- **Nags:** Alarms aren't the only annoying roosters. As teenagers prefer to be lone wolves without parental influence, this personal weapon increases responsiveness. They can also be used in variants such as the digital "MOM Voice" that is now available in HD with unlimited playback options for all your electronic devices, as well as the stealthy sticky notes that prove parents you do *in fact* have eyes in the back of your head.

- **Buckets:** This method is simple but highly effective. As a last resort, strategically apply one full bucket of ice water to sleeping teens.

- **Decoys:** Decoys to hide personal valuables or food stashes. These devices only work if you *remember* where the decoy is hidden. Do NOT leave decoys in open danger zones.

- **Camouflage:** This is a specialized tactic for blending in behind enemy lines. Using specialized camouflage disguises can be helpful for gaining insight and intel.

PRACTICE

Practice use of the Poking Stick in situations such as unre-sponsive teens, large feeding groups, extended periods of game-play, or sanitization of clothing. For more information on the availability of the poking stick, other personal battle gear, or same-day shipping, please

FOLLOW   #NEDSBATTLEGEAR

16

The Safety Gear

Axiom Echo

Do not forget the importance of your personal protective gear to safeguard against certain acts of malarkey, and always remember to **think safety first:**

- **Hard hat**: Useful when there is a potential for injury to the head from falling objects such as eggs, potatoes, pumpkins, fruitcakes, and other airborne projectiles.

- **Eye/ face shield**: An eye or face shield will protect the eyes, nose, mouth, and face from flying debris. There are too many pies and not enough facial shields.

- **Ear Protection**: PPE in mini; these will safeguard against the excessive noise common in teen environments or decibels high enough to cause permanent hearing loss. A must against newly transitioned groupies and falsettos.

- **High Visibility Vest**: A favorite among fashion-forward hipsters from 1974, these are quick to sell out at Neds. Highly visible during night watchman assignments, pantry raids, and recovery missions.

- **Heat protectant gloves:** Used to protect hands during high temperature engagements or when fending off hungry mobs.

- **Steel-toe boots:** These durable boots have protective reinforcement in the toe that protects you from falling objects or bouts of teenage angst.

- **Respirator:** Respirators are especially useful behind enemy lines, sanitizing teen caves and patrolling teenage mayhem. This equipment also protects you from inhaling dangerous substances, such as hazardous chemicals and malodorous cave fumes.

REMEMBER

Always think 'Safety First.'

17

Defensive Positioning

The following are specific tactics that can be useful when playing strategically and engaging daily with your teenagers. These can be used as defensive maneuvers to deescalate hormone surges and put your parental action team in the most effective positions to calmly assist with transitions.

- **Play it Smart**

  - Always Think Ahead. This is crucial. Wildteens can be slippery, and many times have accomplices to assist them in gaining the upper hand. Thinking ahead, recovering intel, and decoding strategy will help you regain control on the battlefield.
  - Know where your safety and protective equipment are at all times

- **Play It Safe**
  - Never confront a Wildteen without a safety partner, someone who is committed to the health and safety of your teenager.
  - Stay near your safety partner at all times when confronting these wild teens or as a safety group if a group is necessary.
  - Samaritan Safety: Pay attention when walking alone or in crowded areas, especially in areas where wild teens are known to congregate. At night, carry a flashlight and wear reflective clothing. The ultra-bright neon and the clothing's reflection will temporarily stun any wild teen. Avoid using electronic devices or wearing earbuds when

walking. The vibrations of a Kenny Lee album will enrage any pack within several miles.

   ◦   Always wash and clean your hands after entering a Teencave or interacting with a teenager. The biological contaminants are toxic to the outside environment. If soap and water are not available, use hand sanitizer containing at least 80% alcohol to ensure proper decontamination.

   ◦   Beware Your Eyes unless you want to lose them!

   ◦   Wear safety goggles or glasses and protect them so you do not lose them during feeding times or gatherings. If you get any toxic substances in your eyes, immediately tell your safety partner and flush with water.

- **Play it Right**
    - Dress for Battle.
    - Wear the appropriate clothes and combat boots necessary for administering food to large groups of wild teens or social gatherings.
    - Roll up long sleeves if necessary, and keep excess hair pulled back.
    - NO sequins, sparklies, spandex, polka dots, suspenders, overalls, kneehighs, furry slippers, or other jigglies that can cause teen anxiety. They may begin to pace, circle about you, huff, and puff until these items are rendered useless. If you only want to distract a wild teen, ensure you have the *appropriate* equipment.

- **Play it Calm**
  - Always walk calmly with your wild teen, do not run. Walking shows that you are in control.
  - When speaking with your teen, remain calm and collected so that you can control the direction of the conversation.

- **Play Defense**
  - Never eat or drink anything around a Tombie. These teenagers turned bloodhounds have an incredible sense of smell. Do not risk your fingers by leaving food items unattended and/or consuming within a one-mile radius.
  - Please take care to consume any food or drink items offered by your wild teen at your own risk. Sealed, canned, and individually packaged products are generally safe to consume; otherwise, use the ten-foot pole method with baked goods.
  - If your teen is stubborn as a mule and you cannot convince them of logic, you may find it most helpful to simply confuse them.
  - A wise old man named Red always recommends, "If else fails, play dead." During extreme panic or excessive mood surges, using the "dead tired" technique in the old chair signals a cease-fire in conflict. Opposing parties may deem this as "old man syndrome" or "parental shock syndrome," but a chair cease-fire during excessive hormonal assaults will allow both parties time to take a pause away from conflict.

REMEMBER

Practice these consistently in order to safely navigate if you are caught in the crosshairs of your wildteen or behind enemy lines.

ON SALE NOW!

Ned's Backwoods Shack is the nations number one trusted source for personal safety and emergency preparedness, and is an excellent choice for restocking your safety equipment. We all know first hand the importance of being well-prepared for any situation, and that's why we partnered with Ned's Backwoods Shack to offer you a wide range of essential parent kits. These parent emergency kits are designed to meet your personal safety needs, whether you are at home or on the run. They include essential supplies and safety equipment to keep you prepared during emergencies. From first aid supplies to emergency tools, the parent safety kits are designed to provide you with survival tools in the event of an occasional cannon strike or Twitch Itch. Order yours today, **supplies are limited!****

18

Rules of Engagement

As active puberty surges into DEFCON, new strategies may need to be engaged by action teams. Generally, during any active engagement, events are subject to additional "rules" of battle. The ILW Rules of Engagement is a general code of conduct that all action teams are expected to know, respect, and obey.

- The ILW Rules of Engagement apply to all teams, regardless of what home team they are on and where they are operating.
- These rules of engagement govern battle tactics and the use of parental bribery techniques.
- Typical rules of engagement for parental action teams that you are likely to see in most battle scenarios are as follows:

- **Acceptable:** Peace-keeping and mood management operations are essential, as is the defense of pantries and supplies from hostile forces in the area.

- **Suggested:** Do not engage or strike out when at all possible. Only act when necessary for self-defense or preservation of supplies. Minimize collateral damage when possible, and enlist the help of family canine units for the protection of perimeters.

- **Restricted:** Do not engage anyone who has surrendered a white flag, is in defiance mode, or is out of battle due to illness or academics.

- **Warning**: Do NOT seize property, including electronics and devices, unless targets are howling in the light of the moon like buffoons. Treat all novice teenage civilians and their property with respect and dignity.

- **Permissible, but *With Caution***: Detain any Wildteens, Tombies, or migrant buffoons caught during acts of malarky or curfew violations. "Grounding" and electronic withdrawal tactics are permissible but used only with caution.

- **Expressly Prohibited**: Looting of Teencaves, lockers, and use of war trophies.

- **Strictly forbidden:** Bribery tactics.

HERE ARE SOME HELPFUL STRATEGIES TO MANAGE MOOD SURGES DAILY AND KEEP YOURSELF IN MORE INFLUENTIAL POSITIONS:

- Engage only opposing forces, random acts of buffoonery, and compromised targets seeking active combat.
- When deployed in a designated combat zone, it is crucial to practice what you preach. Conduct yourself with dignity and honor.
- Comply with the International Law of War. If disgruntled siblings see a violation, they will report it.
- Establish the necessity of using escalated tactics in response to juggernauts. Do not assume the worst, and do not exaggerate. This can escalate conflict, leading to a standoff or worse-Parental Shock Syndrome.
- Attempt to de-escalate mood surges and resolve the conflict without catastrophe when possible. Waging war can be exhausting, especially if you forget the source of the original violations.
- Respond with proportional force— a tactic sufficient to end the hormonal threat and nothing more. You may not have time for stall tactics in the heat of battle or during a standoff. That's why it is essential to think ahead, to prepare both defensive and offensive strategies. During combat training, it is advised to

practice making quick decisions, including survival mode techniques.

- Prepare defensive strategies for situations in which you are captured behind enemy lines or caught red-handed by opposing forces. Understand your boundaries, strategies for reverse capture, and the offensive capabilities of the word "No." To help prepare, practice Survivor Mode and/or Mac Methods.
- Spare academic records when possible.
- Engage Yucatan Mind Meld in specific settings- very effective with those individuals who do not yield to more traditional forms of contract negotiation.
- These ROEs will remain in effect until the governance has consulted the Master Ouija Board for direction.

REMEMBER

If you find yourself in immediate danger of a teenage
takeover, please call the
Emergency Support Hotline.

Survival Notes IV:
Trouble Shooting

19

Survival Mode

Remember, this is a limited-time-only opportunity for you to experience ultimate revenge from your teenager. To fully tackle that hormonal schmooze flowing from your teenager, you should be prepared to focus and practice. The continued exercise of specific skills will help to maximize a survival mindset when surprises come your way- from twitchy teens, smashed fenders, or plundered pantries...

When those hormones strike, don't just sit there cowering in the corner, do something about it! When you start to panic, do something about it! Remember that **you** can manage the panic and fear by managing what is in your areas of control. You cannot control what catastrophe has struck your kitchen, but **you can control how you engage the return.**

You already have a parental toolbox with skills you have learned along the way, without the help of an instruction book. Start adapting your skillset with new strategies that will help you survive when catastrophes attack. Managing your arsenal will help you stay in control of your own actions and engage with honor.

Applying a method called **"Survival Mode"** can be extremely useful in helping you change your attitude from that of a victim to that of a survivor. Survival Mode stems from the body's fight-or-flight response, the instinct that responds to a possible threat. The Survival mode method is less about strategy and more about applying practical skills.

In real-time, this method is used when you must observe the details around you to make practical decisions about the next steps for engaging. Will you panic and flee during random acts of buffoonery? Or will you calmly observe the situation around you, identify the problem you need to address and focus on what action you need to get to the solution? Once you have assessed your environment, you can determine the skills and tools you need to solve your problem without panic. The giant panic button can be conquered; it just takes practice, sweat, and patience.

Practice using this method to play vigilant defense. Look at every tangible item available around you as a possible tool for active engagement. Even the smallest object can be a tool if you hold it and use it correctly, from a paper clip to a pizza box. For additional training on technical skills in the field, refer to the Mac Method of skill under pressure. This will help you build a solid foundation of tools in your arsenal to utilize and not be outplayed during times of duress.

PRACTICE

Be Prepared for any situation, and when in doubt, refer to the Mac Method of skills under pressure. Practice tuning into the skills available to you when engaging "Survival Mode", remain focused, and you will overcome defeat.

20

Do NOT Panic

Without any cheat codes to part the sea through puberty, fear and panic are common emotions that parents face as they journey onward. It is natural to have experienced a stressor during a lifetime event that threatened your ability to remain calm and collected during engagements. Moving forward with any adolescent crisis, it is imperative that the parental action team remain in control and avoid a state of overwhelming panic. Instead of looking at the situation as a crisis, view the situation at hand as a challenge with a solution. Take a deep breath, remain calm, tune into your surroundings, and apply learned skills to the presenting problem. ReWork the challenge without panic, apply your skillset, and engage a solution. ***Panic Button Not Included.*** Remaining calm will help you keep your head attached during foul play.

Applying the "survival mode" technique to your everyday skillset can not only help you stay more tuned into the environment and behaviors around you, but the method can also help you remain in control of your emotions on any battlefield. For extra support, pair skills you already have mastered in your toolbox with your new panic-free techniques to help you be more prepared for more intense engagements.

The next time you go to pound that big red panic button, don't lose your head. Please do NOT panic, let them see you sweat, or let them see fear. If they sense it- game over!

21

Do NOT Shock

Maintaining a balanced composure and managing stress levels will help avoid parental shock syndrome, a state of extreme panic that progresses rapidly into a state of paralysis after an unforeseen stressor. Parental shock syndrome (PSS) can present a very sudden onset in adults, with symptoms ranging from hysteria, headache, loss of vision, confusion, and amnesia.

If you or a loved one has experienced signs of parental shock syndrome, please call a doctor immediately or visit your nearest emergency room. An individual who develops parental shock syndrome will most likely receive supportive care from a treatment team. Treatment could include:

- Management of hyperextended stress levels
- Stabilization of blood pressure
- Fluids treat dehydration, and 160-proof induction therapy is administered as needed.
- Supportive care to treat other signs and symptoms.
- Care plan for home, stress level management, and reduction of future shock and awe symptoms. Some stress management activities include yoga, meditation or other relaxing exercises.
- **Caution**: Parental shock syndrome can recur. People who have experienced PSS in the past are more likely to be susceptible to recurring episodes if they do not seek treatment or use coping strategies to manage stress levels successfully.
- To avoid Parental Shock Syndrome: DO NOT PANIC, remain calm, and do NOT let them see fear!

REMEMBER

PSS in adults can have a sudden onset. Maintaining a balanced composure and managing stress levels will help avoid a recurrence of
Parental Shock Syndrome.

22

Proaction

In support of action plan strategies, practice proactive methods with teens, targeting forward-thinking interventions rather than reactions to crisis. Don't wait until it's too late- make your moves count while interventions are most effective:

- During increased hormonal surges, keep pantries stocked with additional quantities of DingDongs, HoHos, and Chunky Monkey in case supplies are plundered.
- Keep lines of communication open, and remain as neutral as possible. Stay proactive with intel and use tactics to maintain awareness of any associated social activities.
- Encourage healthy hobbies when possible, independent of group activities, to keep mood surges at a minimum. Lion wrangling is currently trending on TumbL, but it is NOT recommended by the USDA.
- Remember that wild teens can react to peer pressure from positive and negative influences; having a positive impact or mentor can help reduce misdirected malarky type behavior.
- Keep your parental radar finely 'tuned in' and operational at all times. Watch for clues of independent or group behavior that seems different than usual. Using this 'radar' sense goes hand in hand with the Survival mode, but the methods are most effective as you become more skilled at 'tuning in'. You can

tune your radar by becoming more aware and observant of your surroundings and then recognizing your reactions. Tune in to your senses of sound, sight, and feeling to get a 'gutsy' read on the environment. Turn up your Beltone, put your readers on, and recheck the emergency guide to Buffoonery. Look at your teenager to observe patterns of behavior. If your radar goes off, it could be something you need to check into.

- Stay proactive with small details, important details that could get overlooked. Sometimes, the small stuff is just as important as the big stuff and can make a huge impact.
- If the radar goes off, please follow up with a professional who can help process any hazards that may have been dropped.
- **Path to Recovery, it's almost there!**

PATH TO **RECOVERY**, IT'S ALMOST THERE!

23

Connections

The experience of peer group connections among teens becomes increasingly important as teens seek more closeness in friendships with whom they can grunt and snarl. Acceptance into the social group, or the Teenpack they run with, is vital to the social strata of the teenage dimension. A teen may modify speech, dress, behavior, choices, and activities to become more accepted by their peers. This increased similarity among peers gives them a sense of security and affirms their acceptance into their chosen pack. Instead of looking to families for sources of support, teens now turn to one another to tackle daily angst and heavy game consoles.

"Just hanging out" is something that teens actually do, with or without parental permission. Instead of fighting the system, parents must get used to the fact that the family dynamics have evolved into a new structure that revolves around a developing teenager. Regardless of buffoon status. This new teenager has evolving needs that constantly change and adapt to the outside social sphere.

If not socializing with the herd, they are likely hibernating in the Teencave or engaging in social networking activities. An increasing trend finds teens focus heavily on the social roads of distraction to fill their needs, regardless of the letters (PS2, X, IOS, META, FB, INSTA, etc).

As teens become increasingly devoted to social scenes, if the activities are removed, it can send teens into shades of shock and awe. Acquiring the latest intel on your teenager's connections will help you make the most informed decisions regarding activities, whereabouts, or concerns.

Remember- under Revised Code 043.201, black market techniques of sneaking, snooping, stalking, and creeping are permissible only when in need of emergency intel. First, attempt to obtain information straight from the source and use bribery only when absolutely necessary.

For quick reference, the most common Teenpack "hang out" activities that parents can monitor for concerns or acts of malarky are listed here:

- Bowling
- Bingo Binging
- Disco Dancing
- Book Bungee
- Geostashing
- Watertubing
- Piefacing
- Funfacting
- Firebreathing
- Swordsmithing
- Ducking
- Festing
- Ear Splitting Cacophony
- Honky Tonks
- Bull Running (Now this does cross over to buffoonery for some)
- Boonies
- Gameapalooza
- Craftcrashing
- Tiktaks

24

Support

It is recommended that action teams support healthy connections for their teens, in addition to their evolving social relationships, in order to:

- Increase positive and more stable emotional patterns.
- Decrease disruptive behaviors and acts of buffoonery.
- Increase lines of communication with peers and adults.
- Learn healthy patterns of social behavior, positive friendships, and mutual relationships with others.
- Demonstrate growing independence, stepping stones to an eventual launch into adulthood.
- Increase positive engagements with parents and support teams. Nurture opportunities for growth and building more positive relationships.
- Turn a social impasse into a possibility.

Continue to keep your radar finely tuned, even with additional supports in place, in case you sense that something seems off with your teenager. It could be small things like a missed outing with the Teenpack, leftover Twinkies at breakfast (WHAT???), or an extra fiery engagement at the dinner table.

There may be a variety of reasons that your teen has barricaded in the Teencave, and may be seeking help. The reasons are various, anything from a social relationship to substance abuse. Whatever the reason- Do NOT Wait! Take even one minute to shed your armor and show your teen that you are 110% in their corner. Show your teen that you are standing by them to give support, even if they aren't ready to talk about it.

It may not happen overnight, but *showing you care in a time of real crisis is the true reason you picked up this book.*

REMEMBER

If you or your Teen are in crisis and need immediate assistance,
please reach out to the
Tombie Support Network at:
info@ihearttombies.com

25

Go Wilde

Teens with more challenging or individual needs may need additional coaching, and extra support from team members. Life coach Mr. Igo Boondock guides these situations, noting, "Parents need to think of challenging behavior as opportunities for family bonding!" (Boondocks, 2042). An informational supplement to this survival guide, "Boondock's Guide to the Wildes," is a deep dive into the wild world of rule breakers and ground shakers. Boondock provides a backdrop to some of the scallywags in the world and sheds some interesting perspectives into the stories behind the stories of risk takers.

The guide looks at the history of wild and unruly behavior and the shift in cultural views on misbehavior. Boondocks covers a lot of helpful information for those looking to resort to "normal " behavior, fit into socially acceptable norms, or create more successful relationships.

Boondock's guide, combined with this survival series, can provide readers with last-resort information when faced with any number of wild questions. Need inspiration to help you face some of these challenges together with your teenager? Look no further! There are opportunities out there in your own backyard, waiting to be discovered, for you and your hormonally challenged loved ones.

For a limited-time offer of only $1977.00, you can find more information at www.boonies.info or at all of your local Ned's Backwoods Bargains.

Survival Notes V: Recovery

26

I ♥ Tombies

NL Riven

Parental action team members are encouraged to find additional support during challenging times from local resources, such as the I Heart Tombies Support Group, that offer local connections within the community. These support groups are safe places to share your lousy dad jokes or peer support who won't judge you on your use of fanny packs. Connecting to local resources, regardless of when you seek support, can also help you to:

- Learn better coping strategies for challenging engagements or experiences
- Manage strategies to decrease stress, anxiety, fatigue, or parental shock syndrome
- Increase networks of local parental action teams and community forums
- Local opportunities for parental bonding through activities such as coupon swapping, buggy pushing, plank walking, and The Chunky Monkey Marathon help to release the inner ninja
- Focus on mental health, self-care, and healthy living
- Trade wardrobe strategies
- Sharpen operational strategies
- Support individual goals. Success is possible!
- Raise awareness and opportunities to support new teens and Tombies collectively.
- Stand together with other supportive group members, all committed to standing strong to making a difference in supporting Tombies everywhere. I Heart Tombies!

REMEMBER

You can laugh, cry, even shout- but in the end, you are still
a parent who cares about
THAT *teenager.*

27

The Boonies

Depending on your view, the roller coaster through adolescence can be anywhere from intensive to thrilling. The Survival Team partnered with life coach Boondocks to launch a three-day boot camp that challenged participants to dive in and discover real-world opportunities (Boondocks, Gatergothim Books, 2042).

Boondocks Bootcamp has surpassed its tenth year of operation and growing yearly. Boondocks campers learn how to take full advantage of their once-in-a-lifetime adolescent experience and simple actions to successfully reach the other side of puberty.

Participation in Boondock's Boot Camp is very selective, but research has shown positive program outcomes. The program's selection criteria include repeated patterns of 'abnormal' behavior, reckless abandon, or an inability to transition to adulthood victoriously.

Due to the extensive amount of material covered in a limited amount of time, the boot camp is known to be intensive but rewarding. There are many Bootcamp survivors who, at one time, had been some of the most challenging wild teens in the community. With the help and intervention of the Boot Camp they have worked through challenges to become highly successful adults.

Survivors of the "Boonies" have noted they feel much more prepared to cope with daily struggles and have learned to apply new abilities to "see the trees through the mud." Boonie reviews have also noted more positive communications with friends or family and are less likely to spew fire during fits of annoyance. Parent campers afterward felt more prepared to cope with ongoing adolescent stressors, raving about the Camp's practical applications of the MeTime and Merlot methods. Take a chance and discover your opportunity, the Boonies are out there!

Don't believe our word for it-

Read the reviews here at
www.boonies.info

28

Five To Thrive

As teens step into adulthood and begin the recovery process, knotty houses can begin to mend. Pantries will become re-stocked, and neighbors can start to emerge from their homes once again. Teenagers actively experience the physical and emotional trials of adolescence, but close ones also feel the weight of hormonal schmooze. Families, friends, educators, and community members are all affected by the hallmarks of adolescence and must work together to help teens overcome challenges.

Always engage thoughtfully, even during peacetime, and pursue meaningful connections to build pathways to success. The hormonal trials are only temporary, but the opportunities to make a difference are limitless.

These last five steps of guidance are active recovery steps to help repair and rebuild after the hardships of puberty.

1. Stand Down

As the waves of hormonal tensions ease and you begin to resume pre-crisis activities safely, you can Stand Down. No plundering of the Teencave, cannons must be stored, and absolutely no tampering with electronic devices. Take a **Stand-Down** posture with your teenager, approaching them with more relaxing body language and tone of voice. Standing Down will not only help to ease the tensions with your teenager, but the hope is that your transitioning teenager will be less likely to put a permanent hex on you.

II. Stand Tall

Stand tall, stand proud. You are a parent who has made it through to the other side, even with a bit of added muck, and that is a massive accomplishment in itself. Every teen and every parent has a unique once-in-lifetime opportunity to experience puberty in all its glory, so give it all you have. It may be loud, grumpy, and even smell like the gym locker room- but that teenager is all yours.

I Heart Tombie. Own It. Proud of It!

III. Stand Together

Grow together, Stand Together. When you feel yourself start falling to the dark side, remember that you are not alone in any of these survival challenges. We all have personal battles that we struggle with, whether we are waging them with ourselves or with the nearest erupting teenager. Each hardship can be considered a unique opportunity for personal growth and a chance to stand together with your family. Not only do you have your team for encouragement, but you are a family, a team that stands together during the good and the bad. Keep building the foundation, strengthen it, and appreciate every success. **Stand together, stand stronger.**

IV. Don't Lose Your Head

Recognize that even though this can be a challenging and rocky path to cross, it is also fleeting. Continue to practice the survivor strategies that help keep you calm in stressful situations and out of reach from the big red Panic Button. Be patient with your teenager, for they are experiencing difficult times. Your transitioning teen is still trying to figure out why circles don't fit the squares, and where that smell is coming from. There may come a point when you postulate the necessity to cryogenically store your teen for safety, of course, until the time when your child can communicate more effectively. If you have tried the suggested techniques in this guidebook and still have a Wildteen that you are concerned about, please make sure to follow up concerns with a licensed practitioner. You may be banging your head against the Teencave door and losing faith in the system, but during those isolated events, please keep your head attached at all times. Take a deep breath, and remember that you **still** have the chance to make a difference to the loved ones in your life **every day.**

V. Always Make Time

There will come a time when your wild teen has successfully managed to break free of the nest cave and landed somewhere south of regret- with or without an empty wallet. That said, your fledgling will leave your safety zone faster than your last paycheck. Since the barbs may have settled a bit, it will be possible to engage in full-sentence dialogues again. This is your time to continue building those relationships and working on Teenspeak conversations. Always make time for a coffee run with a side of seven courses for your foraging teen. No claws on the table, of course. Talk about the weather, the next Plum takeover, or the bad breakup that became a worldwide catastrophe. It does not matter in the slightest what you do, as long as you **always make time**...

29

Words of Encouragement

If you have worked through this guidebook and diligently practiced these strategies, you may have concluded that parenting a new teenager can be more challenging than walking your pet rock. Regardless of what part of the solar system the teenager may have landed. In the end, after all fingers and toes are accounted for, your teen's support team is the only one with the power to ensure that your teenager continues progressing toward a successful future. During the states of hormonal assaults, it can be difficult for both the teenager and the support team to think forward and be goal-oriented- but it can happen.

Recognize the steps you and your teenager have taken to get there- the good, the bad, and the smelly. It may take a village to support your teen through the puberty stage, but you will muck it to the other side with as little collateral damage as possible. Transformation doesn't happen overnight, even with a dose of Mr. Magee's Miracle Cream. (It does, in fact, work miracles on Fido's fine lines and wrinkles!)

As the immediate threat weakens substantially, you can safely resume your pre-crisis activities. Not every day is a catastrophe, and you may be able to discover new opportunities for growth for the entire support team as you rebuild. Sometimes, **it only takes one word to make a difference and one moment to create lasting change**.

• Never Fear

Even though your child may have become a Wildteen, and you fear that all may have been lost, do NOT fear. Do NOT ever give up hope or give up on them. You must and will ALWAYS be a parent who loves them **unconditionally**, regardless of becoming a TEENAGER with individual behaviors and needs. Hopefully, with as little sweat and tears as possible, the TEENAGER stage will pass, and everyone WILL live to see another day. One day, your teenager will thank you, and you will be able to repay their kindness with TEENAGE gremlins (I mean angels) of their own.

Never fear what may come   *# NEVER FEAR*

• Never Give Up

You may win this battle, but the war is never over. As a parent, you will continue to laugh, love, heal, and cry with your child until your last laugh. It may be challenging at times, especially during times of extreme crisis, to keep moving forward. During trying moments, rely on your instincts as a parent to nurture even the smallest of wins, and recognize these successes to give your family the strength to battle on through the hard times. Never give up, continue to strengthen the foundation, and keep building bridges in your own backyard.

If there is one survivor lesson you must never forget, let it be to show unconditional love to your children and family regardless of who, what, where, why, or how sloppy it looks. Your children must mature into adults with the absolute faith that you will **never give up on them and that they will always have a safe road back home.**

All is never lost.   *# NEVER GIVE UP*

30

Lastly

Never **Fear** the new challenges that come your way, and **Never Give Up** on those who matter most in life. I have faith that you will overcome hormonal challenges, and I hope you feel free to share *Words of Hope* with those around you.

NEVER FEAR
NEVER GIVE UP

31

Survival Notes VI:
Afterwords

32

Words of Hope

The *Complete Guide to Surviving THE Teenager* is a lighthearted look at some of those more challenging moments of adolescence when we can seldom find a hiding place to shelter from its storm. Unless you can bury yourself in the sand or under a rock, every individual faces the natural progression of human development. Some can confidently stare down these challenges, while others have a bit more difficulty finding their path. In truth, it can take a village to support the needs of youth who struggle with the hazards of what life throws at them.

Even though we can lightly laugh about *some* shared experiences of adolescence, unfortunately, some of the challenges are very real and devastating to those battling a crisis. Regardless of age, race, or reason, the trend of mental health problems today continues to rise.

Break the Silence: Mental Health and Suicide Awareness

Mental health is an important part of one's overall well being, but too often, it is overlooked or misunderstood. In a world where many face overwhelming stress, anxiety, and depression, it's crucial to recognize that these struggles are real, valid, and worth talking about.

It is okay not to have all the answers, and it is okay to ask for help. Mental health challenges don't define a person, but how we respond to them can shape the recovery. Whether you are personally facing a mental health challenge or are supporting someone who is, understanding the signs of distress and knowing where to find support can save a life.

Warning Signs and What to Look For

- Withdrawal from social activities
- Changes in mood or behavior
- Talking about feeling hopeless or trapped
- Sudden or extreme shifts in personality or habits

If someone you care about is showing signs of distress, reach out. A conversation, even a simple check-in, can make a world of difference. If you are struggling yourself, don't hesitate to talk to someone—a friend, family member, or professional. There is no shame in seeking help.

Become an Advocate

One of the most powerful ways we can all help is to advocate for mental health. Raising awareness, starting conversations, and supporting those who may be struggling are all crucial steps in raising awareness. Small acts of kindness—like checking in and listening without judgment to a family member, neighbor, or friend—can have a lasting impact. It only takes one word of "hello," to start a conversation and let them know you care.

- Advocating for mental health means standing up for those who may not have the strength to speak out on their own. It means creating a community where seeking help is seen as a strength, not a weakness. It means not waiting for someone to ask for help but being proactive in offering support.

Make a Difference

Anyone can take action by supporting organizations that provide mental health resources and crisis intervention. Having learned first-hand the difference advocates can make for families and communities, **a portion of the proceeds from every sale** of this book will be donated to programs that include **Madi's House Inc. and NAMI.** This is one small way we can make a big difference together. Every contribution, no matter how small, helps programs that support those in need.

- If you're looking to make a difference, consider supporting additional initiatives that help provide mental health services, raise awareness, and work to prevent suicide. You can be a part of the solution and *give hope when its needed most.*

Where to Find Help and Support

- Family
- Friends, peers
- Neighbors
- Local mental health counselors
- School teachers or staff members
- Support groups
- Community members
- Church members
- Advocates or mentors
- Online therapy services
- YOU!

1. Helplines

- **National Suicide Prevention Lifeline**
  988 (USA)
  A 24/7 helpline for individuals in crisis, offering free, confidential support for people struggling with thoughts of suicide or self-harm.
- **Crisis Text Line**
  Text HOME to 741741 (USA, Canada, UK)
  A free, 24/7 text messaging service for people in crisis, offering support for anxiety, depression, and other mental health issues.
- **SAMHSA National Helpline**
  1-800-662-HELP (4357)
  A free, confidential helpline for individuals and families facing mental health or substance use challenges, available 24/7.

2. Substance Use and Addiction

- **Alcoholics Anonymous (AA)**
  A worldwide fellowship for individuals who struggle with alcohol addiction. Meetings can be found locally or online.
  Website: https://www.aa.org
- **Narcotics Anonymous (NA)**
  Similar to AA, but for individuals struggling with drug addiction.
  Website: https://www.na.org
- **SAMHSA National Helpline**
  1-800-662-HELP (4357)
  Provides resources for those seeking help with substance use issues, offering information on local treatment facilities and recovery programs.

3. Academic and Career Guidance

- **National Career Development Association (NCDA)**
  Provides resources for career guidance, career exploration, and professional development.
  Website: https://www.ncda.org
- **TeenLine**
  A confidential helpline for teens offering support on a wide range of issues, including school stress and relationships.
  Text or call: 310-855-HOPE (4673)
  Website: https://teenlineonline.org
- **The College Board**
  Offers free resources for students navigating the college application process, including scholarship opportunities and standardized test prep.
  Website: https://www.collegeboard.org

4. Financial Assistance

- **211**
  A nationwide service that connects people with local resources for financial assistance, housing, food, and other essential services.
  Website: https://www.211.org
- **National Foundation for Credit Counseling (NFCC)**
  Provides resources for individuals struggling with debt or financial management.
  Website: https://www.nfcc.org

5. General Disability Resources

- **National Disability Rights Network (NDRN)**
  Provides protection and advocacy for people with disabilities, ensuring they have access to education, employment, and other essential services.
  Website: https://www.ndrn.org
- **Disability.gov (USA)**
  A comprehensive government website that provides information on federal and state programs, services, and benefits for individuals with disabilities.
- **Centers for Independent Living (CILs)**
  CILs offer services that help individuals with disabilities live independently, including peer support, advocacy, and assistance with accessing community services.
  Find a local center: https://www.ilru.org/projects/cil-net/cil-center-and-association-directory
- **Social Security Disability Insurance (SSDI)**
  A federal program that provides financial support to individuals who are unable to work due to a disability.
  Website: https://www.ssa.gov/disability
- **Benefits.gov**
  A government website that provides information on various benefits for individuals with disabilities, including healthcare, transportation, and other state-specific assistance programs.
  Website: https://www.benefits.gov
- **Vocational Rehabilitation Services (State-Specific)**
  Each state in the U.S. has a vocational rehabilitation (VR) program that helps individuals with disabilities find and maintain employment, including job training, career counseling, and job placement services.
  Website: https://www.dol.gov/agencies/odep/program-areas/vocational-rehabilitation

- **Centers for Medicare & Medicaid Services (CMS)**
Provides health coverage for individuals with disabilities, including Medicaid for low-income individuals and Medicare for those with certain disabilities.
Website: https://www.cms.gov

6. Mental Health and Cognitive Disabilities

- **National Alliance on Mental Illness (NAMI)**
Offers support, education, and advocacy for individuals with mental health conditions, including mental disabilities like schizophrenia, bipolar disorder, and depression.
Website: https://www.nami.org
- **Mental Health America (MHA)**
Provides resources for people with mental health conditions, including screening tools, educational materials, and support networks.
Website: https://www.mhanational.org
- **The National Autism Society**
Offers resources for individuals on the autism spectrum and their families, including advocacy, research, and support services.
Website: https://www.autism-society.org
- **Medicaid** Medicaid provides health coverage for individuals with low income, including those with mental health and cognitive disabilities. It often covers therapy, medications, and other health services.
- **Social Security Administration** (SSA) Supplemental Security Income (SSI) and Social Security Disability Insurance (SSDI) are federal programs that provide financial support to individuals with disabilities. Website: ssa.gov

- **State Vocational Rehabilitation Services** Many states offer vocational rehabilitation programs to help individuals with disabilities find and maintain employment. These services can also provide job training, educational assistance, and support in the workplace. Website: rehabnetwork.org
- **National Institutes of Mental Health** (NIMH):The NIMH provides resources on mental health disorders, research, and treatment options. Website: nimh.nih.gov

7. Sexual Assault and Domestic Violence

- **National Domestic Violence Hotline**
  1-800-799-SAFE (7233) or Text "START" to 88788 (USA)
  A confidential 24/7 helpline offering support, resources, and safety planning for individuals experiencing domestic violence.
- **RAINN (Rape, Abuse & Incest National Network)**
  1-800-656-HOPE (4673) or Online Chat
  Provides support for survivors of sexual assault through a 24/7 hotline and online services.
- **Love Is Respect**
  Text "LOVEIS" to 22522 or Online Chat
  Offers support and resources for teens and young adults dealing with unhealthy relationships or dating violence.

8. LGBTQ+ Support

- **The Trevor Project**
  1-866-488-7386 or Text "START" to 678-678
  Provides crisis intervention and suicide prevention services for LGBTQ+ youth.
- **PFLAG**
  A support organization for LGBTQ+ individuals and their families, offering local chapters and online resources.
  Website: https://pflag.org

9. General Support for Young People

- **Big Brothers Big Sisters of America**
  Offers mentorship programs that connect young people with adult mentors to help them succeed in life.
  Website: https://www.bbbs.org
- **National Youth Advocacy Coalition (NYAC)**
  Offers resources for young people, particularly focusing on advocacy and social justice.
  Website: https://www.nyac.org
- **Madi's House**
  Support and activities for young adults recovering from mental illness and trauma.
  Website: https://www.madishousecincy.org

10. Online Support Communities

- **7 Cups**
Provides free, anonymous online therapy and emotional support through trained listeners and therapists.
Website: https://www.7cups.com
- **SAM Foundation of Hope**
Online support programs and outreach for individuals of all ages

11. Government Programs

- **Medicaid** (USA)
A government-funded program offering healthcare coverage, including mental health services, for individuals and families.
Website: https://www.medicaid.gov
- **Social Security Disability Insurance (SSDI)**
Provides financial support for individuals with disabilities.
Website: https://www.ssa.gov/disability

12. Community-Based Resources

- Local churches.
- Community centers.
- School programs and student resources
- Nonprofit organizations provide counseling or support groups.
- Local or national support groups.
- Other community or outreach services.
- To find local resources, visiting websites like **211** can help you connect with nearby services.

There Is Always Hope:

- There is always hope. Never give up, no matter how things may seem. Every day can get better, a step towards a new tomorrow, and there are always people who care. It's never too late to ask for help or to offer support. Together, we can break the stigma surrounding mental health and suicide, and start a conversation that can save lives at any age.

> ## WILL YOU TAKE ONE MINUTE TO MAKE A DIFFERENCE TO SOMEONE CLOSE **TO** *YOU?*

About the Author

The author NL Riven holds a Bachelor's Degree in Psychology and a Master's Degree in Counseling, giving a unique perspective on the complexities of human behavior—especially when it comes to navigating the rollercoaster years of adolescence. With a writing style that blends humor and education, NL's work offers practical advice with a lighthearted twist. The book *Complete Guide to Surviving the Teenage* combines insights with relatable anecdotes to help parents and caregivers survive (and even enjoy) the memorable teenage years.

When not writing, Riven can be found spending time with family, most often with a coffee cup in hand. An advocate for community engagement, NL is also a supporter of local organizations and programs that provide essential help during times of need.

Having witnessed the difference advocates can make for families and communities, **a portion of the proceeds from every sale** of this book will be donated to programs that include **Madi's House**

Inc., the SAM Foundation, and NAMI. Please help make a difference by becoming a supporter and advocate for someone in your life.